Seaside Sleuths
The Bald Head Island Gold Rush

by

Helyn Symons Wisner

Bloomington, IN Milton Keynes, UK

 authorHOUSE

AuthorHouse™
1663 Liberty Drive, Suite 200
Bloomington, IN 47403
www.authorhouse.com
Phone: 1-800-839-8640

AuthorHouse™ UK Ltd.
500 Avebury Boulevard
Central Milton Keynes, MK9 2BE
www.authorhouse.co.uk
Phone: 08001974150

First published by AuthorHouse 01/09/06

ISBN: 1-4259-1097-1 (sc)

Library of Congress Control Number: 2005911251

*Printed in the United States of America
Bloomington, Indiana*

This book is printed on acid-free paper.

To Ali.
May you never forget our adventures
while living on Bald Head Island.

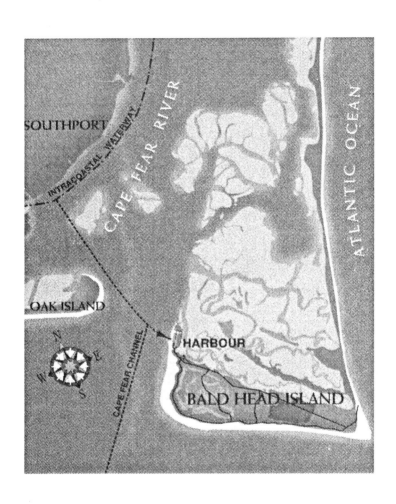

SOUTHPORT

CAPE FEAR RIVER

INTRACOASTAL WATERWAY

ATLANTIC OCEAN

OAK ISLAND

CAPE FEAR CHANNEL

HARBOUR

BALD HEAD ISLAND

"You are now entering Bald Head Island Marina. For your safety please remain on board until a crew member indicates it is safe to disembark. Please keep your hands and feet off the dockside railing as we arrive. Be sure to take all carry-on belongings with you. Enjoy your stay on Bald Head Island."

Ferry Captain

It was a very, very dark night. The wind was blowing eerily and the water lashed ashore with a loud crashing noise. You could hear the breathing of a man running through the reeds. Suddenly the sound of running footsteps stopped and a clang of metal on the ground sounded over and over again. And then, nothing....

Chapter 1

Real Pirate Coins

Many, many, many years later.

"Victor, bring the stick back," yelled Ali. Victor was a jet-black standard poodle and Ali was his eight-year-old owner, a girl who loved adventure. They lived on a tiny island called Bald Head off the coast of North Carolina.

Bald Head is situated on the mouth of the well-known Cape Fear River on the Atlantic Ocean.

Many stories had been told about this famous river and Ali knew every one of them. She, however, had no idea she was in the middle of one of the most amazing stories to take place on this famous river....

It all started this very day.

Ali walked along the beach with her dog, throwing sticks for Victor to fetch as she slowly walked in the wet sand.

All of a sudden, Ali caught sight of something glistening in the sunlight on the beach next to the water's edge. Her mind flashed back to all of the stories she had heard about pirate treasures from shipwrecks years ago on the famous Cape Fear. She had always dreamed of finding treasure near these waters, since many a pirate had sailed along the Cape Fear coast. Even the famous pirate Blackbeard had terrorized these waters.

"Oh I had better quit my daydreaming," Ali said softly.

Still, she walked over to where she had seen the shimmering item, but there was nothing there. Victor barked further down the beach and Ali took off running toward him. She stopped suddenly when she realized he had something in the water. Then she took off at an amazing pace, trying to reach him before whatever he had took off into the water. As she neared Victor she stopped and gazed in amazement. Right there next to Victor's foot was a gold coin! There was no doubt about it!

Chapter 2

The Seaside Sleuths

"I can't believe this is happening!" screamed Ali. "Never, ever did I think I would find REAL treasure. Never." But there it was, right before her eyes. "I must take this back to my house in a hurry," she whispered to herself. Ali quickly gathered up the coin and searched all around the water's edge for more treasure brought in by the surf. Nothing.

Now she turned and raced as quickly as she could back to her home and into her bedroom. "I know exactly who I must contact," she said to herself. "The Seaside Sleuth Club!"

In minutes she was on the phone with a member of the club, which started a chain reaction that made possible the contact of all members within minutes. She knew every member would be gathered at their secret tree within the hour. She must get there. NOW!

The Seaside Sleuths had formed over many summers and was a group of children who lived on the island. Everyone, except Ali, came to the island only in the summer. Ali was the one member who lived there full-time, and therefore, she led the group in their adventures.

All important meetings took place under a huge old tree located outside Ali's house. It was called simply the tree. It was a place where everyone could meet and no one could see or hear them.

Soon Ali heard the footsteps of the first member to arrive. As expected, it was Rebecca Yennek. She was eight also, but could run, bike, surf, and golf better and faster than any kid on the island, including the boys. She had dark hair and freckles and would never, ever be caught dead in a dress.

The next to arrive were the twins Michael and William Strongarm. Michael and William were the jocks of the island, but Rebecca could still give them a run for their money in any sport they chose. Michael and William had great spirits and were game for any adventure at any time. As their name suggested they were very strong and could lift items that were twice their size.

Following the twins to the tree were Casey and James Eflow. They were sister and brother and were very bright. Every year they traveled from New Jersey to spend the summer on the island. They could come up with a solution to any problem at any time. They were simply geniuses.

After a few more minutes, the masters of disguise of the group arrived. They were sisters. Their names were Carson and Wallace Guss. You rarely saw them out of disguise, and today was no different. Carson was dressed in black leather pants and a black leather jacket. She also wore a wig so you had no idea what the "real" color of her hair was. She looked like a biker and no one would have recognized her except for the fact they knew anyone they didn't recognize must be Carson or Wallace. Wallace also wore a bushy, black-haired wig and a pirate costume. Ali had known Carson and Wallace since they were little and they had always, always wanted to play dress-up over any other game, so it was no surprise that they became the masters of disguise of the group.

It had now been more than ten minutes since the first call to the group had been placed. Everyone knew the members on the island would make it to the tree in ten minutes or less if they were on the island. That meant the remaining nine members must be elsewhere. Maybe "off island," as one would say, for trips to Southport, the town right off the island from the ferry ride to the mainland.

Just as Ali was about to address the group, two more members arrived. "Hey, guys," called Josh and Cayla Redes. "Sorry we are late. My dad had to rush to an emergency at the hospital in Southport." Josh and Cayla's dad was a doctor and their mom was a nurse, so Josh and Cayla both were the medical advisors to the group. Any time anyone was hurt Josh and Cayla came to the rescue. Also,

Josh was a great joker and could make anyone laugh, especially Ali.

"Everyone," yelled Ali, "listen to this. Better yet, look at this!" Everyone's eyes lit up with excitement when they saw the gold coin.

"Where did you find it?' asked Wallace.

"On the beach." answered Ali. "It had rolled in with the tide, and I think there are more out there. We had better all spread out and comb the beaches to see if we can find more coins."

Everyone was jumping up and down with excitement. They might actually be finding treasure from the pirate ship that sank years ago in the treacherous waters of Cape Fear. If this was so, they would become rich beyond their wildest dreams.

"Let's go!" yelled everyone together.

"Josh and Cayla, you take East Beach," yelled Ali. "Rebecca, you go with them too. Michael, William, Casey, and James, you go scout out South Beach. Carson and Wallace, you need to go to the ferry landing and listen around to find out if anyone else knows about the coins washing up on shore. Remember, go in disguise so no one will know who you are. That way they will talk more freely around you. Everyone meet back here in two hours," reminded Ali.

Suddenly, two girls and a boy came running to the tree. The girls were sisters Margaret Page and Anna Clainmac. They were members of the group too. Their claim to fame was their singing ability. They could sing more beautifully than anyone in the group and often sang in the island chapel. The sisters were very famous among the "islanders." The boy was Ryan Nihh. He was known as the daredevil and there was nothing he was afraid to try.

"Anna, Margaret Page, and Ryan," yelled Ali, "follow me. We must go check River Beach. I will fill you in on the meeting on our way there."

Everyone took off. If only they could find more coins!

Chapter 3

Busted

Two hours later, the first of the group returned to the tree. It was Josh, Cayla, and Rebecca. Oddly enough, the first to arrive had the farthest to go. They had been to East Beach and now they were exhausted. All of their searching had turned up nothing.

"Do you really think there will be more coins to find?" asked Cayla.

"I don't know," said Josh. "Time will tell."

Just then Michael, William, Casey, and James showed up. They too were exhausted. In fact, Michael was even injured. He had stepped on a sharp shell and his foot was bleeding. Josh and Cayla jumped right on it and began taking care of his foot. After watching their parents and listening to them since they were born, they had a great deal of medical knowledge. First they cleaned his foot, checked to make sure the wound did not need stitches, and then applied medicine and bandaged it. However, before they got to the bandage, Josh teased Michael that they were going to have to stitch the wound up. Everyone jumped on Michael to keep him from running away.

Sadly, though, they too were empty handed. Now everyone was getting discouraged and their hopes were being dashed. They would never find another coin. It had all been just an isolated incident.

Suddenly, they heard running footsteps.

Moments later Ali, Margaret Page, Anna, and Ryan came bursting into the tree area. Not one, but all of them were holding a gold coin. Everyone crowded around them. It must be River Beach where they were washing ashore. No one said anything for a moment. They just stared.

"Okay, now what do we do?" asked William.

"Well, I think the first thing we should do is see if we can find out how old the coins are and what ship they were on," said Ali. "Once we determine that, we can let our parents know and we can all make our announcement. I think Casey and James will be the best for the job. They have such great knowledge," explained Ali. "Let's not say anything to anyone until tomorrow."

"Too late." It was Carson. She and Wallace were just returning from the ferry landing.

"What are you talking about?" asked Ali.

"Three other people on the island have found coins. There is a real frenzy down on the dock. People are just going crazy. Everyone is trying to get back to the beaches. To top it all off, the three people are weekly vacationers," said Carson.

Everyone groaned. Many of the weekly vacationers were notorious for not keeping the best interest of the island in mind. Of course, it was not fair to say every vacationer was this way. All of the members knew the value of the vacationers. Besides, it was a blast to have so many new people on the island in the summer.

"What should we do now?" thought Ali.

Chapter 4

The Bald Head Island Gold Rush

"Casey and James, we still need to find out about the coins," Ali suggested. "See what you can come up with. Tonight is choir night, so let's all meet right after choir practice on the lawn in front of the chapel. Maybe we can come up with our next move then."

Every group member sang in the children's choir in the chapel on the island. Ms. Lorac was their choir teacher and she was loved by all. She also was Ali's piano teacher. Ali and Ms. Lorac shared a special bond and understanding. Tonight would be a good night. Choir practice nights were always good nights.

During the day, the tension and excitement grew as word spread of the coins. The beaches were covered with treasure seekers. It was truly amazing. No one from the Seaside Sleuths made mention of their find. They simply listened and watched the other people.

Choir practice was scheduled for four o'clock. About ten minutes beforehand everyone started on their way. As the members were arriving, you could hear the sound of Anna and Margaret Page's voices coming from inside the chapel. The sound was so beautiful people walking by stopped to listen. The girls were known far and wide for their incredible voices.

As the group entered the chapel, Ms. Lorac cried out, "What in the world is going on? There are people everywhere. I have never seen the island this busy and I have lived here a long time."

Ali spoke first. "Ms. Lorac, gold has been found on the beaches. I mean gold coins. I found one when I was walking on the beach with Victor, and then we found more when the group searched further. We thought we were the only ones but a few of the vacationers found some too. Word has spread and people are going crazy in search of gold coins."

Ms. Lorac was quiet.

Ali spoke again, "We are trying to find out where the coins came from and how old they are."

"I have the information," said Casey. "James and I were going to give you this right after practice."

"Go ahead now," said Ms. Lorac. "This is too important to wait. In fact, I think today we will skip practice. I think things are going to get worse around here before they get better."

"Okay, listen up, everyone," said Casey. "The coins date back to the early 1700s. I can't seem to come up with what ship they were on but I am still looking. I do know this, though: the coins are from the period when the famous pirate Stede Bonnet sailed the waters here around Cape Fear."

"Hey, that's the name of a road here on Bald Head," piped up Ryan.

"Didn't you already know that?" responded James.

"Okay, okay, let's get back to the history," broke in Casey. "Listen to this. It is very interesting. In 1718 Bonnet sailed his flotilla of ships to Cape Fear and anchored to wait out the hurricane season."

"Boy we can sure understand that," said Rebecca. "Think of all the times we have had to evacuate Bald Head because of hurricanes." "Yeah," everyone chimed in.

"Well, word leaked out that there were pirates in the area and the Carolina authorities sent ships to capture them," Casey continued. "Bonnet was anchored in the place now known as Bonnets Creek. A violent fight broke out and Bonnet was captured. I just can't find out if they had treasure on board, or anything to do with the coins."

"Tell them what we found out about Stede Bonnet," said James.

"Well, Stede Bonnet was called the 'Gentlemen's Pirate' because he did not fit the familiar pirate profile. He came from a very productive and prosperous family. No one knows why he chose to go from a gentleman planter to pirate. There has been speculation he was seeking high adventure or he was mentally deranged. Popular legend implies he was escaping a nagging wife."

"What happened to Stede?" asked Josh.

"Well, he was hung in the end," answered Casey. "I think it is more than a coincidence that the coins are from the same time period when Stede Bonnet was near these shores."

"This is creeping me out," said Ali.

Now Ms. Lorac had something to say. "Hasn't anyone thought about the fact that Steve Bonnet, who lives here on Bald Head, has almost the same name as Stede Bonnet?"

"Wow," thought Ali. "For some strange reason, when you get to know someone so well you don't think about their name anymore."

"He is the descendent of the real Stede Bonnet! I guess I never thought to tell all of you. We haven't had much need to talk about pirates in choir, now have we," joked Ms. Lorac. "I think you should all go and see Steve. Maybe he knows something."

The group ran outside and stopped. Helicopters were buzzing overhead. Crowds were running down the street. People were running through the forest, throwing trash and trampling down the brush. Fights were breaking out everywhere.

The sleuths decided to ride their bikes around the island to see what else was happening. First they went to the river in front of Ali's house. People were actually trying to swim across the river from Oak Island. Didn't they know the current was too swift? Others were coming over on jet skis and boats. Anything to reach the island. The beach was covered with people. Thousands. This was terrible. Trash was everywhere. Hopefully they would stay off of the loggerhead turtle nests. The island protected the nests, and the turtles were very dear to Ali's heart.

Next they went to South Beach. Same thing. Nothing was going to stop this.

East Beach was even worse. The group started thinking maybe they didn't want to be rich and famous beyond their wildest dreams. Somehow, some way, they needed to put an end to this.

"That does it," cried Ali. "We need to contact Steve, and fast!"

Chapter 5

The Gentleman

Everyone ran to their bikes and began to pedal as fast as they could. They knew from Ms. Lorac that Steve Bonnet lived on the island road named after his ancestor Stede Bonnet.

As soon as everyone was in Steve's driveway, they all huddled together to make sure they knew what they had to say.

"Okay, let's make certain we find out as much information as we can," Ali informed the group. "We need to know if Steve knows anything about these coins. I am sure he is aware of the ruckus on the island. Let's go!"

Suddenly a man came around the house and approached them. "Can I help you?" the man asked. The startled children took a step back.

"We are looking for Steve Bonnet," Ali replied.

"Oh, he is inside," responded the man. "I am his gardener. Just knock on the door. I am sure he will hear you." With that the man disappeared as suddenly as he had appeared.

Everyone headed up the stairs to Steve's house. Ryan rang the doorbell. No one could hear a thing. Ryan rang the bell again. This time footsteps could be heard, and suddenly the door opened.

Ali recognized Steve from the many times she had ridden the ferry with him. Steve knew Ali immediately, since she was the only child who lived on the island.

"Good afternoon, my dear children," Steve said as he greeted them. "It certainly is my pleasure to welcome you all into my home." The group crowded into the entrance of Steve's home.

"We really don't mean to bother you," Ali started to say.

"Oh nonsense," Steve replied. "This is such a pleasure to have all of you as visitors. Please come into my living room and I will have my housekeeper bring all of you some fresh lemonade."

Ali started to protest, but everyone looked eager for the refreshments, so she went along and followed everyone into Steve's living room.

"Mr. Bonnet, we are here because we are afraid the island is being destroyed," Ali began. "I am sure you are aware that the visitors to the island have reached epic proportions and it is all due to the coins that have washed ashore. Everyone is thinking they will be the one to find the treasure and become rich. People have gone crazy! The island is being destroyed!"

"Please, please. Don't get yourself so worked up," Steve said calmly. "I am certainly aware of the events of the past few days, but I am not sure I can do anything to help. Is there something more I should know about?"

"Well, Ms. Lorac told us you were a descendent of the famous pirate Stede Bonnet," Rebecca explained. "We know the coins came from the same time period in which Stede Bonnet sailed these waters."

"We thought maybe you could tell us if your ancestor had stolen treasure and hidden it somewhere in this area," piped in Josh. "Everyone knows the rumor that Blackbeard has treasure hidden somewhere in these parts, and we thought maybe Stede had done the same thing."

"I am afraid I won't be able to help you," sighed Steve. "Not much about my ancestor has been passed down in my family except for the name. You probably know more about him from your research than I do. It's a funny thing. I guess when the history is in your own family, you get tired of hearing it."

"Well, okay. We just thought, if you did know something, maybe we could stop the island from being destroyed," Ali responded. "We thought if you knew he had definitely NOT buried treasure, we could tell everyone and they would go home. We will not bother you any longer."

"Nonsense. Your visit is such a pleasure," Steve replied smoothly. "Now please enjoy the lemonade." With that the housekeeper entered with the refreshments.

Helyn Symons Wisner

Chapter 6

Now What?

"I didn't like him!" whispered Cayla to the group as they left Steve's home.

"Are you crazy?" cried Josh. "He was as polished as the real Stede Bonnet. He was a real gentleman."

"Something wasn't right. I swear it," Cayla said in a hushed voice.

"Cayla may be right," Ali agreed. "I just don't know. But I do know we're not going to get any information from him."

"What should we do next?" asked Anna. "We can't just give up."

"Well, the way I see it, either there is a real treasure or someone is planting the coins to cause all of this commotion," Ali surmised. "I think we need to put a watch on all of the beaches and I think we should start tonight. Let's all go back in our original groups to each beach and watch secretly. Meet at the tree in the morning. Nine o'clock sharp!"

With that everyone took off!

Chapter 7

Evil

The man was all alone. He had a determined look on his face.

"Those measly, rotten kids. Can't they leave well enough alone?" he muttered to himself. "I would like to take every single one of them and ship them off the island this minute."

With that thought, he pulled on his boots and started for the beach. As night engulfed the island, a thick fog rolled in and an eerie silence hung in the air.

"I will take care of them. If not tonight, I will get them tomorrow. They will wish they had never gotten involved in this," he muttered again to himself.

Chapter 8

A Very Eerie Night

"Boy it sure is scary out here," whispered Margaret Page.

"I don't like it," agreed Ryan.

Margaret Page, Ali, Anna, and Ryan were all huddled together on River Beach, trying to keep an eye out for anyone who might come to the beach. Since darkness had descended, all of the treasure seekers had left and the beach was abandoned. It was becoming increasingly difficult to see down the beach, since a fog had been rolling in the past few hours.

"How much time do we have left?" asked Anna.

"Just about one more hour," answered Ali. Everyone's parents had made it clear they were not to be out past 11:00, and that time was drawing near.

"I will be glad when we get out of here," Anna whispered. "This place is creeping me out too."

"Wait!" Ali cried in a hushed voice. "Look down near the point." Everyone turned in that direction. There, right on the point, was a hazy figure. You could see him bending down. It really looked like he was putting something in the water.

"Victor. Attack!" Ali yelled.

With that command, Victor took off. The figure turned in their direction and within seconds had disappeared into the night. They ran as fast as they could, but the stranger was nowhere to be seen when they arrived at the point.

Victor was whining and pawing at his eyes. It appeared that whoever the figure was had sprayed something in Victor's eyes to keep him from attacking him.

Ali knelt next to Victor and hugged him close. It was already apparent that the spray was wearing off and Victor would be fine.

"That jerk!" cried Ali. "He must be very evil to do something like this to an innocent animal, let alone Victor."

"What do we do now?" asked Ryan.

"Look around and see if you can find anything that might give us a clue as to who it was," shouted Margaret Page. "Maybe he dropped something."

"Well, you are right about that," Anna said as she pointed to something on the sand. "Look here. There are more coins. It certainly looks like he has been planting them here, for some reason. Now we just need to figure out why. Maybe that will lead us to him."

"Why do you keep saying he?" Ryan asked. "You know we were not close enough to tell if the figure was a guy or a girl."

"Okay, okay. Let's look a little further," said Ali.

"Well, well, I would put my bets on it being a guy," cried Margaret Page. "Look!" Margaret was pointing to a footprint in the sand.

Sure enough, there were several very large prints in the sand. A few were leading away from the water's edge, probably to where he had gone once he realized he had been spotted. They gradually became so faint you could barely see them. But the ones you could see were large. Very large.

"These are certainly not your average woman's shoe size," announced Ryan. "There is no doubt that Margaret is correct. The figure was most definitely a man!"

"Well, this is a start," encouraged Ali. "Look how unusual the print is. It had very large grooves on the sole. I bet it is some kind of work boot."

"He certainly had a lot of traction to make a fast get away. He would not have run unless he was up to no good," Anna pointed out.

Helyn Symons Wisner

Chapter 9

Arrested!

Ali had been waiting at the tree for about fifteen minutes. It wasn't like anyone to be late. "I guess they were all up late last night," she said to herself.

Suddenly Josh burst into the opening. "You must hurry, Ali. The police have arrested Steve Bonnet for planting coins on the beach. They are taking him to the ferry right now. Jump on your bike."

Ali and Josh had never pedaled so fast in their lives. They made it to the ferry landing in record time. All members of the group were already there. Josh had seen them on the way to the tree and they had all rushed over.

All of a sudden, the police car pulled up. Steve Bonnet was taken from the car and guided toward the ferry. He was in handcuffs, something you rarely saw on the island. You could tell he was very upset.

As he passed the children he cried out, "I didn't do anything. I promise you I didn't." His voice grew louder and he pleaded, "Please, someone believe me. Please. Please help me. I would never do anything to hurt this island."

He started to cry, but the police rushed him onto the ferry and down below in a separate compartment so no one could see him any longer.

"Whew. That was pretty bad," shrugged Cayla. "I told you I didn't like him."

"I don't know," Ali said in a puzzled voice.

"What are you talking about?" Rebecca asked.

"I think I believe him," replied Ali. "There is just something about the way he sounded."

"Oh come on," said Michael. "The police found the exact coins all over his house. He lied to us about not knowing anything. That is evidence enough."

"I just don't know. Something seemed so desperate in his cry. He really did not seem like he was acting to me. Let's just ride our bikes by his house before we go home. Come on," Ali said.

Everyone took off and soon they were close to Steve's home. The police had already roped off the area so no one could get near.

"I have an idea," suggested Ali. "Let's come back later tonight and take a look around when no one else is here."

"We can't make it tonight," said William with regret. "Our parents were upset that we were late last night."

"Okay. Can the rest of you make it?" asked Ali.

"Count us in," chimed in everyone.

Helyn Symons Wisner

Chapter 10

One Scary Night

As the children walked up Steve Bonnet's driveway, they felt an uneasy calm. It seemed unusually dark and hot. There was a rustling noise to their right. Cayla jumped.

"Probably a raccoon or deer," Casey said in a hushed voice. Everyone knew the island was full of both animals.

"Maybe so, but it still made me jump," Cayla whispered. "After all, this is where the criminal lived."

"What are we looking for anyway?" Rebecca asked.

"Maybe me," a gruff voice answered.

Everyone jumped and fell back. There, in front of them, was Steve Bonnet's gardener under the light coming from the house's windows.

"W-w-w-w-what are you doing here this late?" Ali asked, trying to sound calm.

But then she noticed his feet. More important, his shoes. They were big. Very big. With heavy soles. Her heart sank.

"That is absolutely none of your business," he growled back. "I am going to keep all of you from nosing around again. You just couldn't leave well enough alone."

Sensing danger Ali yelled, "Run!"

But it was too late. The gardener sprayed something in the air and the children grabbed their eyes in pain and began coughing, trying to catch their breath. One by one the gardener tied them up and took them under the pilings of the house.

"I will figure out what to do with you before morning. I just need a little time to think," the gardener said, more to himself than anyone else.

Cayla scooted over to Ali. Fear was in her eyes. "What are we going to do?" she whimpered. Tears started to flow from her eyes. Ali wasn't sure if they were from the spray or from fear.

"We will think of something," Ali reassured her. But what, she didn't know. It must have been the gardener all along. But why? How did he get the coins? Maybe she could get him to talk and could stall him.

"Have you been planting the coins all along?" asked Ali.

"Yeah, yeah, yeah. You might as well know. After I ship you off this island, you won't be able to use any information against me. Anyway, the police have arrested Mr. Bonnet. I am free and clear."

"But why? Why would you even care about planting the coins?" continued Ali.

49

"Are you kidding? More people mean more business for me. I just didn't plan on everyone and his brother going mad, thinking they were going to get rich. The minute I saw those coins of Mr. Bonnet's, I knew I could bring a lot more people to this island. But everything got out of hand, so I had to set Mr. Bonnet up before they found out about me," the gardener explained. He actually looked a little sad. "On the other hand, I don't care if they trash this island. Some of these people here have been treating me like dirt, no pun intended. And you kids drive me crazy, always messing up the gardens, running here and there. You kids wanted to get rich too. Go ahead and admit it. You wanted to be the first to find the coins."

Everyone knew he was right. At least they had put the welfare of the island first.

"So not only did you cause the mass destruction of the island but you stole valuable coins from Mr. Bonnet," Ali surmised. "What are you planning on doing with us?" she demanded.

"Nothing," a voice from behind them cried out. There, standing only a few feet away, were three policemen and Michael and William.

The gardener started to run but he was quickly grabbed and thrown on the ground. They had handcuffs on him within seconds.

"We heard everything," stated the captain of the force. "I think you owe Steve Bonnet a big explanation. Let's go." With that they carted him out to their police car and they were gone.

"What in the world are you guys doing here?" screamed the group as Michael and William untied them.

"We begged our parents to let us come too," Michael explained. "We told them this would be one of our last adventures before we left the island for the summer. Finally they let us go, but when we got here we heard one of you cry out, so we crept up and saw what was going on from behind the bushes. Of course, we took off and found the police, and you know the rest of the story."

"You will be our heroes forever," everyone cried out. "Let's get out of here."

Chapter 11

Summer's End

Summer was coming to an end. Today all of the children were leaving on the four o'clock ferry. Some would go to Raleigh, some would go to Charlotte, and some would go to New Jersey. They were from all over the country.

Steve Bonnet had been released from jail. He was very grateful to the children for searching further, resulting in both the real culprit being apprehended and his release. He had thrown a party for the children on East Beach and had given each one of them ten coins for their bravery. He told them he had lied about knowing anything about his ancestors because people had hounded him for money over the years when they found out who he was.

Everyone understood, since they had seen firsthand the destruction that could come from the thirst for treasure.

The island had been cleaned up and restored to its natural beauty. It would take a few years to get it totally back into tiptop shape, but they had come a long way. The whole group had worked very hard to clean it up and they took great pride in the way it looked.

"See you next year," cried Ali as she waved to the ferry. She and Victor ran down the path leading to the pier that ran along the entrance to the harbor. There they could stand for one last good bye before the boat left the harbor. All the children were standing by the boat's railing.

"See you next summer, Ali," everyone cried above the boat's motors. And then they were gone.

Chapter 12

It Can't Be

"One last walk before school starts," thought Ali. "I sure miss my friends, but I will see my school friends soon."

Ali was headed down the beach with Victor by her side. The sun was shining and the air was getting cooler. "Thank goodness," Ali thought to herself. The summer had been very hot and the cool air felt good.

Ali waved to Ms. Lorac, who was on the beach with her husband, Mr. Nod. They waved back. "I think I will go back home by the marsh," she decided.

As Ali started down the road next to the marsh, she picked up a stick and threw it. It went a little off course and landed in the reeds in the marsh. Victor's eyes followed and he dashed off into the reeds, eager to fetch. Ali waited but Victor did not return.

"I guess I better see what is up," Ali said to herself. She turned off into the reeds and walked in the direction of where she had seen Victor enter the marsh. As she approached Victor she could see he was digging in the ground. She thought he was after a crab, but soon realized it was something different.

She knelt down and felt goose bumps go up her spine. There before her eyes was the brass handle of something below the ground's surface. She didn't want to let herself think what she was thinking. She grabbed a large stick and began to dig. Finally she had the top attached to the handle all cleared off. It clearly was the lid of something. She ran to the road and stopped an approaching golf cart. She begged the driver to help her and they ran back to the site where she had been digging.

"Please help me lift this lid," she cried out. With a swift tug the lid was off!

"Glory be!" cried the driver.

Ali fell to her knees. There before her was a chest full of the most wondrous treasure. Not only gold coins, but also jewels … necklaces, rings, and bracelets.

"This is the real thing," she said calmly.

The man cried out, "You are rich!" He grabbed her and lifted her into the air.

"No, no, no, noooooooooooooooo!" cried Ali. "This treasure goes straight to the museum!

About the Author

Helyn Symons Wisner has lived on Bald Head Island for the past four years with her daughter, Ali; her husband, Jim; and their dog and cat, Victor and Rainbow.

Printed in the United States
42459LVS00001B/91-183

9 781425 910976